You Wonder

⇒ All the Time ⇐

Deborah Farmer Kris

Illustrated by Jennifer Zivoin

free spirit
PUBLISHING®

Library of Congress Cataloging-in-Publication Data
Names: Kris, Deborah Farmer, author. | Zivoin, Jennifer, illustrator.
Title: You wonder all the time / Deborah Farmer Kris ; illustrated by Jennifer Zivoin.
Description: Minneapolis, MN : Free Spirit Publishing Inc., [2022] | Series: All the time series | Audience: Ages 2–6
Identifiers: LCCN 2021039507 (print) | LCCN 2021039508 (ebook) | ISBN 9781631986987 (hardcover) |
    ISBN 9781631986994 (pdf) | ISBN 9781631987007 (epub)
Subjects: LCSH: Curiosity in children—Juvenile literature. | Questioning—Juvenile literature. | BISAC: JUVENILE
    FICTION / Imagination & Play | JUVENILE FICTION / Social Themes / Self-Esteem & Self-Reliance
Classification: LCC BF723.C8 K75 2022 (print) | LCC BF723.C8 (ebook) | DDC 153.3—dc23/eng/20211217
LC record available at https://lccn.loc.gov/2021039507
LC ebook record available at https://lccn.loc.gov/2021039508

Free Spirit Publishing does not have control over or assume responsibility for author or third-party websites and their content.

Reading Level Grade 1; Interest Level 2–6;
Fountas & Pinnell Guided Reading Level I

Edited by Cassandra Sitzman
Cover and interior design by Emily Dyer

10 9 8 7 6 5 4 3 2 1
Printed in China
R18860222

Free Spirit Publishing Inc.
6325 Sandburg Road, Suite 100
Minneapolis, MN 55427-3674
(612) 338-2068
help4kids@freespirit.com
freespirit.com

FSC
www.fsc.org
MIX
Paper from
responsible sources
FSC® C144853

In memory of my boundlessly
curious father, Jim Farmer, who
always loved my questions

Who, what, when, where, why, and how?
Can I please? Why not?

You ask amazing questions and
you ask them quite a lot.

You wonder all the time.

"Why does the moon grow big and round, then shrink to just a sliver?"

"When I get out of the steamy tub,
why does my body shiver?"

You wonder all the time.

"Why do sliding snails make slime?
Why do some bugs sting?"

"Where do our snowpeople go
when the weather warms in spring?"

You wonder all the time.

"What will happen if I drop
an egg onto the floor?"

"What will happen to my tower
if I add one block more?"

You wonder all the time.

"Why are flips called *summer-salts* instead of *winterpeppers*?"

"Do I have to put on shoes?
Can't I just wear slippers?"

You wonder all the time.

"What if we traveled back in time
to meet some dinosaurs?"

"What if we rode a T. rex
and shook the forest floor?"

You wonder all the time.

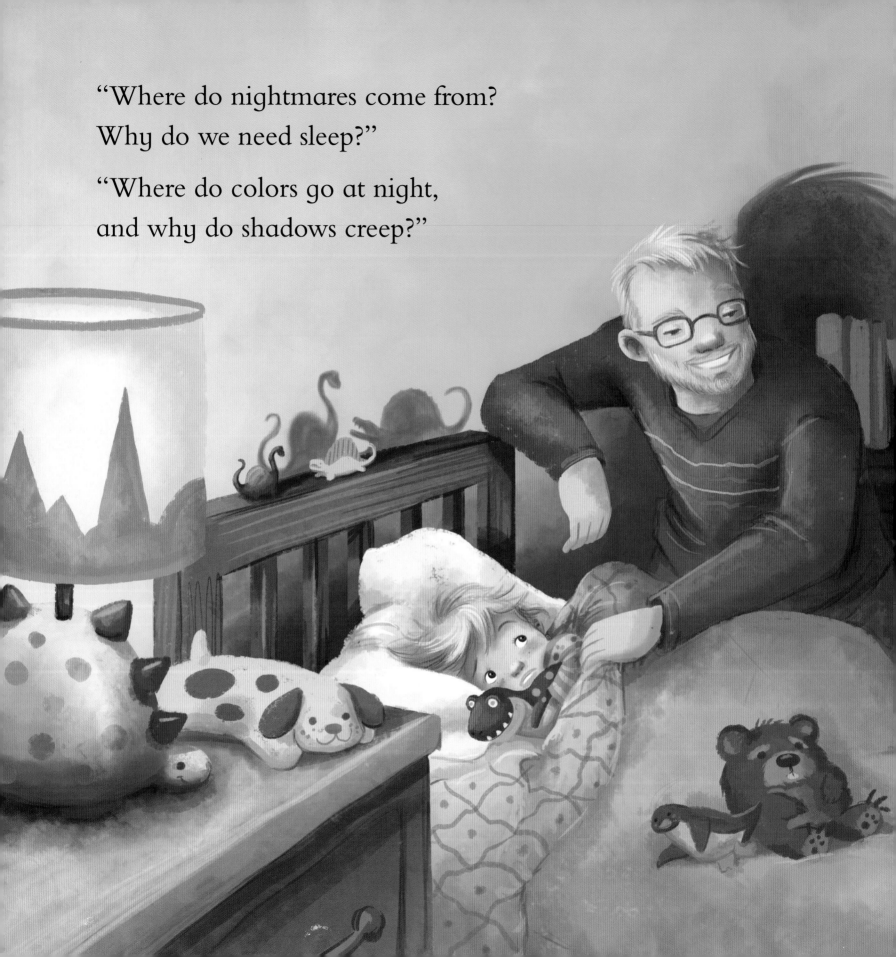

"Where do nightmares come from?
Why do we need sleep?"

"Where do colors go at night,
and why do shadows creep?"

You wonder all the time.

"Why do people's skins
come in different shades?"

"Why do I have short hair while
my best friend has long braids?"

You wonder all the time.

"Why don't dande*lions* roar?
Why do old leaves crunch?"

"Who invented candy canes?
What will be for lunch?"

You wonder all the time.

"Why do nodding heads mean yes
and shaking heads mean no?"

"Why do grown-ups stop the fun
and say it's time to go?"

You wonder all the time.

The world is full of questions,
so I will ask one too.

Will you stay curious as you grow?
It's a brilliant part of you!

You wonder all the time.

And if you ask a question
that I simply cannot answer,

we'll think it through or look it up—
we'll find it out together.

We wonder all the time.

A Letter to Caregivers

One day, when my daughter was four, I wrote down all the *Why?* questions she asked in a single afternoon. They included:

- Why can't I drink water and breathe at the same time?

- Why do slugs make slime?

- Why are they called hot dogs if they aren't made from dogs?

- Why don't dande*lions* roar?

- Why does the sun go to bed later in the spring?

Children's constant stream of *Why?*, *Can I?*, and *What if?* questions can sometimes test the patience of parents and caregivers. But our kids are wired to explore, label, and make sense of their world. And that's a good thing!

Wondering is a form of curiosity. When we ask questions, we are using our observation and reasoning skills. When children are curious, they are not only motivated to learn, but they also learn more effectively. As psychologist Craig Anderson told me, the more wonder and awe children feel, the "more curiosity they express and the better they perform in school."

Here are five ways you can nurture children's wonder and curiosity.

1. Enjoy Nature Together

Spending time in nature is one of the best ways to elicit wonder in children. But you don't need to head to the Grand Canyon or see the Northern Lights to experience the magic of the natural world. Go for a walk, letting children set the pace as they stop to dig in the dirt, jump in leaves, or search for treasures. Explore a local farm, park, or Audubon center. Go to an open field to observe the night sky. Turn over stones to see what creatures live beneath. Identify the birds, plants, and insects that live in your neighborhood. Being in nature not only stimulates children's brains, it supports their emotional well-being too.

2. Explore Cause and Effect

One of my favorite questions children ask is often an unspoken one: *What will happen if . . . ?* This is a great scientific question that helps kids learn about cause and effect.

Of course, this question can also be the cause of mess and stress as children wonder, *What will happen if I drop this egg on the floor?* or, *What will happen if I flush my toothbrush down the toilet?* When necessary, try redirecting their experiments without squelching their curiosity. If they want to know what happens when they turn the juice carton upside down, let them play outside with cups and a jug of water. If they want to know what it's like to draw on walls, mix up some bathtub paint (you can find a recipe online) and set them loose in the tub. In other words, try saying, "You can't do that, but you can do this!"

You can also ask *What if?* to set up simple, cause-and-effect science experiments such as these:

- What will happen if we drop food coloring in the pancake mix?

- What will happen if we sprinkle salt on this ice cube?

- What will happen if we build the sandcastle closer to the waves?

- What will happen if we drop the acorn and the leaf at the same time, and from the same height?

- What will happen if we add a paperclip to the nose of the paper airplane?

- What will happen if we plant one seed in the sun and the other in the shade?

3. Let Them Figure It Out

Giving children explicit instructions for how to play can limit their creativity and their discoveries. For example, when you show children how to use a toy, they are more likely to play with it in only one way: the way they were taught. However, when you let them figure it out on their own—particularly with open-ended toys such as blocks—they get curious and are more likely to find new and creative ways to play. Some of the most *wonder*-ful toys come from the recycle bin: think paper towel tubes and cardboard boxes.

4. Listen and Find Answers Together

One way to support children's wonder is to simply listen to their questions. It feels good when people pay attention. And when we honor children's questions, we validate their curiosity and invite them to keep exploring.

When children pose a question we can't answer, here's a powerful response: "That's a great question! Let's find out." Experiment together. Look up the answer in a book or online. Call a friend or family member who is an expert. All these responses show children that their questions are valued, demonstrate tools they can use to find answers, and encourage them to keep questioning and wondering as they learn and grow.

5. Model Wonder

Children take their cues from us. When we get excited about learning something new, experimenting with a new recipe, or investigating the nest we spot in a tree, we remind them that wonder is a lifelong pursuit.

Take children to the library and pick out books about diverse topics that spark your interest and theirs. Even if you don't read the books before you return them, flipping through pages filled with pictures of dinosaurs, ocean life, pyramids, or cute baby animals can expand children's knowledge and prompt new questions.

You can also inspire children's curiosity by wondering out loud yourself: *The clouds are getting darker! I wonder if rain is coming? I wonder what bird is making that noise? I wonder why the moon looks so big tonight?*

As Dr. Dacher Keltner, director of the Greater Good Science Center, shared with me: "When I think back on my own parenting experiences, some of the best moments are moments of awe. How do you find awe? You plan unstructured time. You wander. You take a walk with no aim. You slow things down. How do you find awe? You allow for mystery and open questions."

In other words, life is better when we wonder . . . all the time.

—Deborah Farmer Kris

About the Author and Illustrator

Deborah Farmer Kris is a child development expert and parent educator. She serves as a columnist and consultant for PBS KIDS and writes for NPR's *MindShift* and other national publications. Over the course of her career, Deborah has taught almost every grade K–12, served as a school administrator, directed leadership institutes, and presented to hundreds of parents and educators around the United States. Deborah and her husband live in Massachusetts with their two kids—who love to test every theory she's ever had about child development. Mostly, she loves sharing nuggets of practical wisdom that can help kids and families thrive.

Jennifer Zivoin has illustrated more than forty children's books, and her art has appeared in children's magazines, including *High Five* and *Clubhouse Jr.* She illustrated the *New York Times* and #1 *Indiebound* best seller *Something Happened in Our Town.* The Children's Museum of Indianapolis, the world's largest children's museum, featured her art in a special *Pirates and Princesses* exhibit. Jennifer provided artwork for celebrity picture books, including those by James Patterson and Guns N' Roses. Recently, Jennifer made her debut as an author with her book *Pooka & Bunni.* Jennifer lives in Indiana with her husband, daughters, and pet chinchillas.

Great Books from Free Spirit's All the Time Series

Written from the perspective of an adult speaking to a child, these whimsical rhyming books help young children know that they are deserving of love through life's ups and downs. This encouraging series shows them all the ways they're supported as they continue to grow and learn. *32 pp.; color illust.; 10" x 10"; ages 2-6*

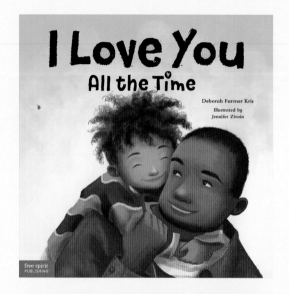

For pricing information, to place an order, or to request a free catalog, contact:

Free Spirit Publishing Inc. • 6325 Sandburg Road • Suite 100 • Minneapolis, MN 55427-3674
toll-free 800.735.7323 • local 612.338.2068 • fax 612.337.5050 • help4kids@freespirit.com • freespirit.com